To Sail Beyond the Sunset

Write-ups about some places that I loved

Swapna Dutta

Ukiyoto Publishing

All global publishing rights are held by

Ukiyoto Publishing

Published in 2022

Content Copyright © Swapna Dutta

ISBN 9789360164805

All rights reserved.
No part of this publication may be reproduced, transmitted, or stored in a retrieval system, in any form by any means, electronic, mechanical, photocopying, recording or otherwise, without the prior permission of the publisher.

The moral rights of the author have been asserted.

This book is sold subject to the condition that it shall not by way of trade or otherwise, be lent, resold, hired out or otherwise circulated, without the publisher's prior consent, in any form of binding or cover other than that in which it is published.

www.ukiyoto.com

Dedication/Acknowledgement

Footloose at Neuchatel, Annecy: A Medieval Town Where Time Stands Still and St. Albans: A 2,000 year-old City were first published in Scottish Home & Country. Sunlight on the Piazza was first published in The Pioneer. Barnet: On a Literary and Historical Quest and A Peep At Paradise were first published in Deccan Herald.
In the Land of the Singing Waves was published in Scottish Home & Country. Legendary Pushkar was published in Young World (The Hindu). Before the Cosmic Dancer, Magical Madikeri, Nainital: A Hill Station Among Lakes and The Shelter of Two-and-a-half Days were published in Deccan Herald.

The book is dedicated to all who love to travel.

Foreword

My Scottish Editor Liz Ferguson had once told me that a travel piece can be considered a success only if it wants to make the reader wish to visit the place. I assume it also implies that the piece itself should be interesting enough to do this, even without the aid of photographs. She had accepted several of my pieces for the magazine she had been editing then, *Scottish Home & Country*. However, my newspaper editors, for whom I have been writing for a long time, insist on photographs as well. No matter who the piece is meant for, for me one thing is of prime importance – I cannot write about a place unless I am moved by it, either because of memories or interesting legends associated with the place or something I feel to be significant. In some cases hot tourist spots leave me cold while a neglected corner makes me feel that it is well worth writing about.

To Sail beyond the Sunset consists of 12 write-ups about places I have visited and loved. It is in 2 parts. The first is about places outside India while part II speaks of places in India. They describe my personal impressions and feelings and do not claim to be an all-inclusive fact file. But I sincerely hope that if my stories interest my readers they will visit the places and find out whatever else I may have left out.

Contents

Part I	1
Footloose at Neuchatel	2
Annecy : A Medieval Town where Time Stands Still	6
St. Albans : A 2,000 year-old City	10
Lindau: An Island in Lake Constance	13
Sunlight on the Piazza	16
Barnet – On A Literary and Historical Quest	20
A Peep at Paradise	23
Part - II	28
In the Land of the Singing Waves	29
Before the Cosmic Dancer	32
Legendary Pushkar	35
Magical Madikeri	38
Nainital: A Hill Station Among Lakes	41
The Shelter of Two-and-a-half Days	45
About the Author	*48*

Part I

Footloose at Neuchatel

I caught my first glimpse of the Neuchatel Lake from the train window while travelling from Paris to Geneva. It looked vast and remote, stretching for mile after mile reflecting the dusky blue sky. There were not many buildings along its lonely shore, no crowd of swimmers and sunbathers or colourful boats with sails. Yet something about the place drew me irresistibly as we shot past and I decided to return some day and get to know it better.

We made it at last on a July morning when it was pouring with rain. Unfortunately there is no way of knowing beforehand what the weather is going to be like when planning a journey weeks in advance. One just has to take what comes. As we made our way to the hotel, wrapped in raincoats, in what felt like a regular deluge, my only fear was, would the boats ply on the lake in this weather? It would be too, too bad if it didn't! It was one of the first things we enquired after getting into dry clothes and refreshing ourselves with steaming cups of tea. Luckily a boat trip was scheduled for the evening. That gave us practically the whole day to explore the city. Luckily the rain stopped as suddenly as it had started and a listless sun peered out of the clouds. Good enough, I told myself as we stepped out of the gate.

"Neuchatel" got its name from a structure built as a stronghold during the Burgundian rule in 1504 when the place belonged to the French Orleans-Longueville family. It passed on to Prussia in 1707 because the people chose Frederick I of Prussia to be their ruler. Finally Neuchatel became part of the Swiss Confederation in 1815.

The canton is charmingly located between the lake and the Chaumont Hill. Nestled at the steep foothills of the Jura Mountains, it has a gorgeous view of the Alps. The town is on the northern shore of the lake. Most of the houses are pale ochre in colour, a fact that made Alexander Dumas remark that the town was "carved out of a pat of butter". It stands in the middle of vineyards which stretch all along the lake. In fact, vines have been cultivated on the Neuchatel hillsides for the last 10 centuries. The grape harvest is celebrated here with a colourful wine festival. Neuchatel is renowned for its excellent red wines and the fruity "Œil-de-Perdrix". The white wines are made from the Chasselas grapes that grow here abundantly. Neuchatel wines have several elegant specialties, which include sparkling wines and Chardonnays.

There is an "old world feel" about Neuchatel which continues to wear a medieval look even today. As we strolled along the cobbled streets we saw time-worn picturesque houses dominated by fountains and towers. Two buildings –the church, La Collegiale Notre Dame and the Castle – dominate the scene. The church is a striking 12th - 13th century Roman-Gothic building with multi-coloured glazed tiles. I particularly liked the high, star-covered ceiling and the exquisite stained glass windows. Originally a Catholic church, it was converted in 1530 as a result of the Reformation. Parts of the original building were destroyed in a big fire in 1450. It was majorly restored during the 19th century.

The Castle, originally the residence of the Neuchatel lords, is now the office of the cantonal government. The buildings are grouped around a large courtyard. It still retains some of the 12th century features. One of them is the Romanesque gallery in the southwest wing that has seven blind bays. We were told that the castle had been re-built several times. The prison tower has three distinct levels belonging to three different periods. The lower part is said to belong to the 10th century, the middle level to the 13th century and the uppermost parts to the 15th century.

Just below the castle stands the Hotel du Banneret, built in 1609, which is a typical Renaissance town house of the time. There is a richly decorated fountain in front – Fontaine du Banneret – with a statue on top carrying armour. It was created by Laurent Perroud. The locals pointed out yet another interesting building, the Hotel Du Peyrou. It was built in the 18th century for a financier named Du Peyrou, a friend of Jean-Jaques Rousseau, the philosopher. The hotel – graceful and distinctive - stands in a garden which feels special because of a beautiful relic from the past – a statue standing in a pool of water known as "The Bather".

After our jaunt through the Old Town we ambled towards the lake, passing by several shops. Seeing the colourful array of chocolates everywhere I remembered that Neuchatel is famous for chocolates too, especially truffles. We stepped into a quaint little shop. I had heard that Neuchatel chocolates are mostly hand- made. I asked the owner of the shop if the claim was true. "Oh yes" he replied promptly, "they are all made by hand in small batches. They are hand-decorated and hand-packaged as well."

"Why would you say that the Neuchatel chocolates are different?" I asked again, reading the colourful ads on the walls, some of them in English. "It's the cocoa beans that make the difference" he replied, "our chocolates are made from the finest cocoa beans and you find nearly twice the amount you'd find in ordinary chocolates." We ended up buying quite a lot of chocolates as gifts and munched some with great relish as we continued our walk.

Another sight not to be missed is the Nauchatel Natural History Museum. We had already heard that the Lake Neuchatel is joined to Lake Biel and Lake Murten by canals. That is why the area is generally known as the "Three Lake" region. This entire area used to be the heart of the Iron Age culture known as La Tene (c 500 BC–0 BC). In the 1870s, the eastern end of the lake dried up and many objects belonging to the period were dug out. They have a special character of their own and are known as "La Tene art". Among these finds are the remains of a yoke, which can be dated to 200 BC. All these finds are now housed in this museum which makes it quite special. At least I had not come across such exhibits before.

At last we were at the lake for the boat ride I'd been eagerly waiting for. The jetty seemed totally deserted. There was not a single soul around. Nothing but ducks, swans and seagulls floating gracefully along the fringe of the lake. We were the only two passengers aboard, though another family joined us on the way. I was disappointed that I could not see the Mont Blanc and the Bernese Oberland Ranges because of the low clouds. Normally one can see both clearly from the lake. Nevertheless the cruise was exciting enough as we cut across the dark waters with a strong wind blowing. We learned from the big map on the boat that the first steamer had plied on this lake in 1827.

Lake Neuchatel is the largest lake in Switzerland. Lake Constance and Lake Geneva are bigger in size but they are shared by neighbouring countries and do not belong to Switzerland exclusively. Being 38 km long, 8.2 km wide with a maximum depth of 152m, the lake owes its origin to a former glacial lake in the Aare valley at the base of the Jura Mountains and is mainly fed by the Zihl River. Other rivers which also flow into the lake are the Orbe, the Arnon, the Areuse and the Seyon.

Since we had merely been nibbling chocolates all this time we greatly enjoyed a meal of fresh fried fish and chips, salad and huge glasses of iced tea on the boat. We were told that the lake was simply "teeming with fish". Chocolates were also on sale including Truffles. I was happy to see that they also had a large selection of sugar-free truffles such as Milk Champagne Truffle, Dark Champagne Truffle, Milk Chocolate Truffle, Dark Chocolate Truffle, and Caramel Truffle, said to be every bit as delicious as the ones made with sugar. But they are more expensive, of course.

Our boat touched various ports such as Grandson, Saint-Aubin-Sauges, Cortaillod, Colombier and St. Blaise, picking up or dropping passengers. Some of these places were connected to the jetty by wooden bridges, with flowering creepers entwining the railing. But there were not many people this afternoon. The forsaken waters seemed to belong to the ducks, swans and gulls.

Suddenly the clouds lifted and we held our breath as we caught a fleeting glimpse of the majestic Mont Blanc and the Oberland Range. Then it was dark once again. After a while it started raining. As we reached the landing after nearly two hours and we trudged back to our hotel in the rain I told myself that this was a trip I'd never ever forget!

Annecy : A Medieval Town where Time Stands Still

It was during a visit to Geneva that I first heard of Annecy, a fascinating medieval town in the French Alps. My Swiss friend described it as one of those magical places where time stands still. As it was on the other side of the Swiss border and it was possible to reach there in a few hours by bus I decided to check it out for myself.

"But do you speak French?" asked my friend anxiously. "It's the only language spoken there."

"I can say 'please' and 'thank you'. I shall manage, don't worry," I replied confidently. I knew from past experience that not knowing the language of the place could never be an insurmountable problem.

I had quite forgotten my fear of heights, however, and as the bus slowly made its way up the steep mountain path the next morning, I felt my feet turning to jelly - aggravated by the fact that the bus was being driven by a lady! I solved the problem by keeping my eyes half shut until we reached our destination. I knew that I was missing out on gorgeous scenery but there was nothing else to be done. When I alighted from the bus I realized that the journey had been well worth it. I was in one of the most charming alpine towns I had ever visited, situated near a spectacular sapphire lake surrounded by glorious mountains. In fact, the place is totally dominated by the mighty Mont Blanc.

The little town of Annecy grew around an 11th century Benedictine monastery around the river Thiou on the edge of the lake. The Thiou canal, the natural outlet of Lake Annecy, flows through the heart of the town. Part of the old ramparts and gateways are there still. As I made my way towards the old town I looked with interest at the cluster of medieval buildings laced with canals, flower-covered bridges, narrow but picturesque arcaded streets and town gateways.

The Thiou Canal winds through the old town, passing cafés and restaurants that were now ablaze with colourful flowers. Annecy is often called the "Venice of Savoie".

Two of the major sights that must inevitably strike every visitor are the formidable 12th Century Palais de l'Isle and the turreted Chateau d'Annecy. The Palais de L'isle, a triangular building shaped like the bow of a ship, is built on an island in the middle of the Thiou Canal and looks as if it is floating there. It is said to be one of the most photographed buildings in France. Originally the City Prison, the building now houses exhibitions. I went round the place admiring the exhibits. Going down the dark and gloomy dungeons is a chilling experience even now and I heaved a sigh of immense relief as I stepped out into the sunshine once again.

The Chateau d'Annecy which blends into the mountain scenery stands out like a signal on the horizon. I found it quite a climb although not a tiring one. I had a splendid view from the top, overlooking the rooftops of the town and Lake Annecy. The chateau has four impressive towers. The Perrière Tower dominates the lake, while the Saint Paul and Saint Peter Towers face the town. The massive Queen's Tower is the oldest of them all, having been built in the 12th century.

In 1394 the chateau became the official residence of the Counts of Geneva and remained one until the end of the family line. It now houses the Museum of Annecy. The defensive wall is surmounted by a parapet walk. It was here that my camera got stuck. And I realized with dismay that more than 'please' and 'thank you' was needed to save the situation! I tried to act out my problem to the amused French visitors and luckily one of them understood what I wanted and came to my rescue.

After a much needed cup of coffee at one of the cafes I made for the lake. Lake Annecy is the second largest lake in France and has the reputation of being "Europe's cleanest lake". It was formed nearly 18,000 years ago during the era of the large alpine glaciers. It is fed by many small rivers from the surrounding mountains and also from a powerful underwater spring, le Boubioz, that gushes out at a depth of 82 meters. The blue-green waters of the 23-mile -long lake, reflecting the snow-capped mountains and dark green forests, has been admired by many famous artists and philosophers such as Cezanne and Jean-Jacques Rousseau, who spent several years here. I discovered during my walk the Jean-Jacques Rousseau Square that has a small basin cut out in an alcove containing the bust of the great philosopher. There is also an inscription that says that this was the place where Madame de Warren whom he called "maman" had her little house. Annecy is also full of churches. Notre-Dame-de-Liesse Church is known for its Roman bell-tower, slightly leaning. Saint Francois Church, St. Peter's Cathedral and St. Maurice Church are some of the others.

The place is popular for water sports, such as sail-boarding, diving, rowing and water-skiing. And it is great for fishing as well. There is a charming cycle track built on the line of a disused railway line which runs for almost the entire length of the lake shore. People come here all the year round for snow skiing. Tignes, a popular ski resort, is just 150 km from Annecy. Die-hard sports enthusiasts can also get plenty of rock-climbing, para-sailing and hang-gliding. The promenades bordering the lake were full of boats but I realized regretfully that there was no time for a boat ride since I had to return to Geneva the same evening.

Luckily I had landed up on a Friday, one of their market days. The entire Old Town was filled with booths set up by vendors selling fresh fish, vegetables, flowers, pork products, a wide variety of cheese and pots of honey. Savoy is famous for its cheese-based dishes. I tried their Tartiflette, made of alternating layers of sliced potatoes and cheese, baked with cream, onions and herbs. Delicious, though not particularly suitable for weight-watchers! The famous fondue Savoyarde is a mixture of cheese melted in garlic and white wine. But what I liked best of all was their Friture de perchettes which is crisp-fried perch fish, fresh from the lake.

But not all of Annecy is medieval. As I stepped out of the narrow cobbled streets of the Old Town I was face-to-face with modern buildings, boutiques full of designer clothes, night clubs and cyber cafes. I also heard that Annecy is the venue for the Annual Animation Film Festival. But if you turn away from this little modern segment, Annecy does seem like an enchanted land that belongs to another time, another place. A magic realm where the past mingles with the present like a harmonious duet.

St. Albans : A 2,000 year-old City

I looked around curiously as I alighted at the city centre of St. Albans. I was at the oldest town in Hertfordshire, a settlement over 2,000 years old and the location of many significant events.

There are shopping malls on every side giving the place a hep and contemporary look. But it is the magnificent Abbey Cathedral situated at the centre of the historic city which dominates its skyline. As I made my way towards it I recalled what the place has stood for all these years.

The town, originally known as Verlamion, which means 'the settlement above the marsh', belonged to the Iron Age. After the Romans conquered Britain in the 3rd century it was renamed 'Verulamium' and became one of the largest towns in Roman Britain. Alban lived in this city and worshipped Roman gods like the others. But he became a Christian later and refused to give up his faith despite severe torture. Finally, his execution was ordered. Alban was dragged out of the town, across the river Ver and up a hill (now known as Holywell Hill) where he was beheaded. According to legend, a spring of water miraculously appeared on the hill-top to give the would-be martyr his last drink. According to another version, a well sprang up where his head fell after the execution. The eyes of the excutioner are said to have fallen off the moment he beheaded Alban. Thus St. Alban became the first Christian martyr of Britain. The legend of St. Alban is a remarkable one and was recorded by venerable Bedes, a noted scholar of the times. The place has been a shrine for Christians ever since and pilgrims flock here from far and wide to pay their tribute to St. Alban.

After the Roman army departed in 410 AD Verulamium turned to ruins. But soon a new town grew around an abbey established by one of the Abbots. It was close to the place where St. Alban had been martyred and was named "St. Albans" in his memory.

St. Albans is also historically significant. It was, at one time, the principal abbey in England. The first draft of the Magna Carta was drawn up here in 1213. The place played a major role in the Peasants' Revolt in 1381. Fifteen of the rebels were tried at the Moot Hall, the site of the present Town Hall. St. Albans sided with the parliament during the English Civil War (1642-45). Later Cromwell was said to have chased a royalist sheriff right up the Holywell Hill where he was captured and imprisoned in the Tower of London.

Located on a grassy hilltop above the city, St. Albans Cathedral is breathtaking in its size as well as grandeur. Its architecture is a blend of many different periods and its great tower has several Roman bricks salvaged from the ruins of Verulamium. The north arcade is made of original Norman pillars. Many of them retain their old murals, depicting crucifixions, saints and similar subjects. The south has mainly Early English Gothic structures.

I particularly remember the huge lantern vault under the tower, decorated with colorful coats of arms. The actual shrine of St. Alban was smashed during the Reformation. It was later reconstructed from more than 2,000 fragments scattered all over the Cathedral. The Abbey Gateway was used for many years as a prison. It now forms part of St Albans school and the Cathedral is a busy centre for church-related as well as cultural activities.

The next structure, in order of importance, is the Clock Tower. Built between 1403 and 1412, it is one of the only two medieval belfries in England that is still in existence. Built by the people of the town as a symbol of their independence from the church, it has survived 600 years of use. But the location is rather crowded now.

The ancient Clock Tower not merely sounded the hours but was also used as a curfew and fire alarm. Its bell rang for the first battle of St. Albans during the War of the Roses in 1455. I was told by the tourist guide that Donovan, the popular singer, learnt to play the guitar outside the clock tower.

Other sights in St. Albans include the Verulamium Museum which displays magnificent mosaics and recreated rooms of the Roman period. A short walk away is the Roman Theatre, said to be the best preserved one in Britain. It was originally used for bear baiting and cock fighting. It is also ideally suited for musical and dramatic performances because of its fine acoustics. Our guide pointed out a 16th century house which was the home of Francis Bacon, the famous philosopher. Finally we walked up to the Kingsbury Watermill, also constructed in the 16th century. Its wheel, once damaged, has now been restored and we saw it churning the water of the River Ver.

St. Albans' close proximity to London has made it a popular locality for shooting films and serials. Some episodes of *Inspector Morse* were shot in and around the Abbey Gateway and school grounds. *Life Begins* was also largely filmed there. The Lady Chapel of the Abbey was the location for Sean Connery's film, *First Knight*. *Birthday Girl* and *Incendiary* were both filmed in St. Albans.

And yet, despite all the shopping malls displaying the latest brands and the contemporary crowd I came across on the streets, once inside the Cathedral premises I could feel the peace, tranquility and serenity of centuries. It is easy to understand why it continues to remain a much-sought-after place of pilgrimage.

Lindau: An Island in Lake Constance

The sky is overcast with clouds as our train chugs along the little bridge that takes us to Lindau, an island in Lake Constance. The causeway meant for cars joining the island to the mainland is on the other side. This rail causeway was built way back in 1853. The dusky sky blends with the dark water far away making the lake seem boundless. The English call it Lake Constance, the Germans call it Konstanz and to the Austrians, it is the Bodensee. The lake is on the River Rhine at the foot of the Alps and belongs to all three countries. Lindau, the tiny 0.68 square-km island that nestles under the Pfander Mountain, is located near the meeting point of the Austrian, German and Swiss borders. It is a part of the German state of Bavaria.

Our train comes to a halt and we look at the tiny station curiously. It feels like rolling into somebody's drawing room! The platform is a part of the main station hall which has seats and shops and flowers everywhere. It is also full of Hallowe'en pumpkins as the popular festival is just a few days away. Our hotel is close by so we decide to walk up there with our suitcases. The cobbled path glistens with raindrops and there is a strong wind blowing. We pass by several manor-style houses, a big church, a museum and parks full of rain-drenched flowers before reaching our destination. We freshen up, drink cups of steaming tea and go out exploring despite the drizzle.

Visiting an island is always exciting. More so, if it is an island in a lake. We decide to start with the harbour, the most imposing sight of Lindau. As we near the place we gaze enraptured at the sight that meets our eyes. There is the huge statue of a lion overlooking the lake on one side and a 33-meter-high lighthouse on the other, flanking the harbour entrance. This is the only lighthouse in Bavaria. The lion, also a characteristic landmark of Bavaria, was created by the famous sculptor Johann von Halbing. We are told that one can climb to the top of the lighthouse for a small fee to enjoy a spectacular view of the lake and the island. We decide to try it the next morning. The harbour as we see it now (people call it the new harbour) was also built in 1853, the same time as the railway bridge.

Lake Constance was formed by the Rhine Glacier during the ice age. This 63 km long and 14 km broad lake provides fresh water to many cities in south Germany. The lake actually comprises three parts – the Obersee, which means, the Upper lake; the Untersee, or the lower lake and a connecting stretch of the river Rhine called the Seerhein. The lake is colloquially known as the Swabian Sea.

Lindau has an interesting history. The name "Lindau" was first mentioned by a monk from St. Gallen in a document belonging to 882 AD. St. Stephan's, the oldest church on the island, was founded in 1180. Later a monastery was founded and Lindau became an Imperial Free City under King Rudolph I. Much later, after many ups and downs and many changes of powers, Lindau finally became a part of Bavaria, Germany.

It is nearly 6 PM. The rain stops and the sky clears up. The harbour lights are on, illuminating the whole place. Suddenly the whole place looks like the backdrop of a fairy tale. Skillfully restored buildings of yesteryears are lit up and cast their magical spell on the visitors. Crossing ferries with glittering lights add to the charm. Until the middle of the 19th century there used to be a night-watchman here who walked around the town by nightfall. He was the custodian of order and security. There is someone now to play that role, equipped with a halberd, horn and a lantern. One can walk along with him on a 90-minute tour through the town and imagine the Lindau of days gone by. But we are too tired to do any more that night. The lakeside is full of cafes and restaurants. We drop into one of them for an early dinner.

We see a different face of Lindau as we come to the charming old town centre the next morning. The past comes alive as we walk through the alleys and discover moments of historical splendour. There is the beautiful Pulverturm (1508) and the Diebsturm (1370) which were once parts of the ancient city wall that protected Lindau and its citizens. We are now at the Market Square. It is a Saturday, the day for collecting fresh produce – cheese, meat, fruits and vegetables

– and is chockfull of people buying and selling. We now head for the Lindau museum, originally built as a private residence. It is full of impressive furniture from Gothic to baroque style; exquisite articles in silver, glass, tin and ceramic; historical toys; beautiful paintings and sculptures.

Lindau is a veritable mecca for those who love water sports, be it swimming, surfing, yachting or boating. Boats can also be hired quite easily. There are conducted boat rides where you get to visit 3 countries (Germany, Austria and Switzerland) in a single afternoon. Lindau is also the meeting place of the Nobel Laureates every year.

We spend the rest of the day strolling around the place, passing several churches. They look old but many have newly constructed towers. The parks are full of flowers. We picnic inside one of them, sitting at the edge of a fountain, watching butterflies. We pass by the causeway for cars, colourful with lots of flags, on our way back to the hotel. As we bid adieu to Lindau the next morning we know that this visit would find a place among our most cherished memories.

Sunlight on the Piazza

Venice as a place has intrigued and fascinated me ever since I can remember. In my early school days it was because of *The Merchant of Venice*, a hoary favourite with most schools, especially the scene where Portia confronts Shylock. Later, as I graduated to school stories, Venice assumed a fresh significance because of *What Katy did Next*. Those of you familiar with the title would remember how Ned proposed to Katy in a gondola on their last evening in Venice. I considered it most romantic during my salad days and envied Katy more than I cared to admit! But it was after being introduced to Byron's *Venice* and Browning's *In a Gondola* during my university days that I learnt to think of Venice as the epitome of romance and longed to see the place for myself. Perhaps there are many others who feel the same.

As I gazed at the shimmering blue of the Adriatic Sea on a sultry July afternoon, ready to step into a 'water bus' which would take me to the heart of the city of canals, I wondered why some people had told me that the water in the canals was muddy and that it stank. The pale blue water looked deep but certainly not murky. All I smelt was the usual sea odour one finds near any other sea shore. There had been a raging storm the night before, followed by a regular deluge. But this afternoon the sun beamed down on a calm waterfront. Venice, I was told, is made up of a cluster of 119 little islands on the Adriatic Sea. I wondered if I would find it quite as beautiful as I'd always imagined it to be.

I need not have feared. Unique, exquisite and fantastic, Venice continues to be enveloped by an aura of romance even now. An air of nostalgia clings to the city with its maze of palaces, calli, canals and the hundreds of hump-backed bridges like a veil of enchanted mist. I felt it as I walked along the Piazza San Marco which had arcaded palaces on three sides. What really stands out is the magnificent Basilica of San Marco. St. Mark had died in Alexandria but his relics were later brought over to Venice by two merchants. The church which houses the same relics was built sometime in the 11th century with extensions, renovations and restorations which continued right up to the 15th century. The facade, of the church lavishly decorated, is surmounted by four gilded bronze horses. The five golden domes of the church gleamed in the sun.

Inside the church I was struck by the splendid Byzantine mosaics which spread from floor to ceiling. The ones near the top still glittered though the ones near the floor were dull with dust and grime. These mosaics were designed by the 12th and 13th century craftsmen. They had been partially restored during the 16th and 17th century with designs created by Titian, Tintoretto and Veronese, among others. The arches which support the intricate domes are beautiful too.

Our guide took special care to point out the Vault of Paradise which contains Titian's *Last Judgement* and the Pala d'Oro, a 10th century alter-piece studded with gems, gold and enamel. It looks something like our own *meenakari*. The treasury which comprises the right arm of the church has an array of Byzantine art pieces - a veritable feast for the connoisseur! One can take a closer look at the mosaics on the vaults if one goes up the atrium of the basilica past the first floor galleries.

The other attraction on the piazza is the tall and stately bell tower. The marble Loggetta at the base of the tower was designed by Sansovino in 1540. It was used as a meeting place for the nobles during the Renaissance. The guide informed us that the tower was rebuilt in 1912 after the original collapsed suddenly one July morning way back in 1902. One can go up the tower in a lift for a breathtaking view of the city. I shivered as I suddenly realized that this was a July morning too! But fortunately the tower stood firm and I had my fill of the view.

Facing the bell tower across Piazza San Marco is the clock tower known as Torre dell'Orologio. It was built a few years after Christopher Columbus discovered America. The clock is a handsome one with a face of gilt and enamel with two figures striking the hours. There is the Napoleonic wing at the end of the piazza which was added in 1810. It now houses the Correr Museum which has exhibits which bring alive the history of Venice.

A trip to Venice is incomplete without a gondola ride. The gondola swayed precariously as I stepped in and made for the middle seat. The July sun blazed down on the shimmering Grand Canal. The sky was a clear, limpid blue with strands of puffy clouds floating by. The 'serenader' in the next gondola sang 'Come back to Sorrento' in Italian to the music of a piano-accordion. Apparently a gandola ride in Venice also includes the serenade. The familiar tune sung in a clear, rich baritone cutting across the water sounded wonderful. The sight of the piano accordion made me feel nostalgic. No one seems to play it anymore! As we threaded in and out of canals the guide pointed out the various important buildings.

I made my way to the Piazetta which opens onto the lagoon. There was Libreria Marciana, a remarkable piece of 16th century architecture by Sansovino, to my right and the majestic Palazzo Ducale to my left. The latter used to be the residence of the Doges who were the elected dukes of Venice. Part of it was also used by the highest ranking magistrates of the city. Built between 1309 and 1442, it is said to be a perfect example of Venetian Gothic architecture. The elaborate portico and the pink and white marble facade look majestic even now. The beautiful courtyard inside leads to the Scala dei Giganti (stairway of the giants) which is guarded by huge statues of Mars and Neptune. The palace is full of exquisite artworks and rich decorations. One of the main attractions is the Scala d'Oro (the golden staircase).

The Bridge of Sighs, which arches over a narrow canal, stands between the east wing of the palace and the Pazzi prison. As the prisoners walked across this bridge to the damp, dark cells below they took a last look at the world outside. Hence the name. There have been several illustrious as well as infamous people among the prisoners.

I walked under the Clock Tower into the Mercerie which is Venice's busiest shopping centre. The street was lined with shops selling the latest designer clothes, jewellery, shoes, leather goods and every kind of fashion accessory, all of them exorbitant and quite out of my reach. Shopping wasn't among my list of priorities, in any case. So I window-shopped casually while walking up to the church of Santa Maria Farmosa built in 1492 which houses the famous painting of Santa Barbara by Palma il Vecchio. The piazza of the church was once used as an outdoor theatre. A little beyond Santa Maria is the Palazzo Campiello Querini-Stampalia, a 16th century palace housing the paintings of Bellini, Tiepolo and Longhi.

A day is too short a time to do justice to the entire Piazza San Marco which is full of interesting palaces, churches, museums and shopping arcades. As I sat on the steps of the Piazza it was fun to see the round of hectic activity that went on inside the enormous courtyard full of pigeons, tourists and people, selling all kinds of ware in wheeled carts. There were ice creams and popcorn; sweets and balloons; toys, T-shirts, caps and what-have-you. All the sellers seemed to do brisk business. Open air restaurants were full of tourists sipping drinks as live orchestras played heady music. It was difficult to imagine that the city of Venice is under a shadow or that its days are numbered. The only message that came across the sound of music, din and laughter echoing all along the Piazza was – 'All's right with the world!'

Barnet – On A Literary and Historical Quest

I am standing in what was once called the Great North Road in Barnet, looking up at the Red Lion (originally spelt Lyon) Inn. Except for the figure of the lion way up above, it looks like any other modern building now. I try to imagine what it must have looked like in the early 16th century when this ancient inn "not only stabled 18 pairs of horses but also boasted of uniformed servants", something unique in those days! This picturesque borough in Hertfordshire is a collage of open green fields; blossoming parks ablaze with colour; lakes full of swans and ducklings; tranquil old churches set against ancient shady trees; quaint inns; and quiet avenues lined with pretty villas and blooming gardens. But I am here today primarily on a literary and historical quest. What I mean to explore is the Barnet of Charles Dickens, Dr. Johnson, and Samuel Pepys; the Barnet of Georgette Heyer and the Barnet of King John, Henry VIII and John the Baptist.

Coming from London, you would run into the High Street, choc-a-bloc with shops and shoppers like any other busy street, and wonder where on earth the history lies buried. But step into any lane that leads to the quiet countryside and you would know where to look. Originally known as Chipping Barnet, the word *Chipping* means the presence of a market, set up in the 13th century which continues to this day. King John is said to have granted the charter for the market more than 800 years ago. At the center of the town stands St. John the Baptist Church, built around 1250. I stepped inside to see the medieval nave and aisles separated by clustered columns, which support four pointed arches, a vestry, built during the reign of James I and a low, square embattled tower, all of them beautifully maintained. Other churches in Barnet - St. Mark's, St. James's and St. Mary's and others - stand out like little islands of tranquility.

The historic Barnet Fair that dates back to 1588 was visited by celebrities and commoners alike. This naturally led to the building of several inns on the Great North Road. It soon became a popular stopover point for famous visitors, including members of the royal family. The *Red Lion* is said to be the oldest among the existing ones. Samuel Pepys, Charles Dickens and Ballantyne (Remember *The Coral Island?*) had dined or stayed there. Pepys mentions in his famous diary the cheesecakes he had tasted here. Dr. Johnson and Lord Torrington patronized *The Mittre*. Henry VIII's favourite was *The Antelope*. Between 1750 and 1800 magistrates held their meetings in a number of these inns, mainly *The Red Lion, The Mittre,* and *The Boar's Head* (now called *The Crown and Anchor*).

Those of you who remember *Oliver Twist* would also remember that Fagin had first met Artful Dodger at Barnet. Fans of Georgette Heyer would recall the Great North Road that was used for curricle races, elopements and mock hold-ups. Many of her characters stopped by at *Potter's Bar* or *Mitre's Inn* or put up at the *Red Lion*. I felt really thrilled to think of the characters who continue to be prime favourites with many.

Barnet has been the scene of many historic events. The Watling Street (now known as the A5), built by the Romans in AD 43 was the main link between London (then Londinium) and St. Albans. The Battle of Barnet in the War of the Roses (between King Edward IV and the Earl of Warwick) was fought here in 1471 and saw the return of the exiled King Edward to England.

The Barnet Museum is worth a visit for the wealth of information it offers about the Barnet War and the striking paintings of a bygone era. Also on display are centuries-old household objects and costumes dating back to the medieval times. Interestingly, as more than 3,000 people had died in Barnet's Monkden Hadley, it is said to be the second most "haunted village" in the UK, especially famous for the ghost of a medieval knight galloping across the Oak Hill Park in full armour in the company of fellow-spooks. So the place was once named the *Ghosts' Promenade*. Unfortunately I could not see them in broad daylight! I guess most people have forgotten the name as it is a beautiful park now.

It is now time to look for another interesting site for which Barnet was once famous. In 1661 Rev. Childrey published a book, *Natural Rareties of England, Scotland and Wales*, where he mentioned the "Physic Well of Barnet". The water of this spring well was said to be medicinal, as good as that of Tunbridge or Epsom. The most-quoted reference was made by Samuel Pepys in his diary. On July 11, 1664 he visited the well for the first time and drank five glasses of water. He wrote, "The woman (attendant) would have me drink three more, but I could not." Again on August 11, 1667, he reached the well at seven o' clock in the morning and found, despite the severe cold, "many people a-drinking" the water of the well. Daniel Defoe (Remember *Robinson Crusoe*?) also mentions "The mineral waters of the Barnet Well".

But although I located the place easily I could not get to see the well itself. The building in which it is housed is now closed from all sides, probably to protect it from over-inquisitive eyes. I was told that in the 17th century the area used to be a part of the Barnet Common. Although a little disappointed, I didn't really mind not seeing the historical well. The green canopy of the trees, the clear blue sky above and the profusion of flowers all around more than made up for what I had missed!

A Peep at Paradise

I held my breath as the plane touched down on what looked like a few yards from the vast blue Indian Ocean, its foamy breakers touching the edge of the runway. I gazed at the sea in wonder. I had never come across such a glorious combination of turquoise, azure, sapphire, jade and amethyst before, blending so delightfully with the vivid blue of the sky. I was in Mahe, the largest and the most important island of the Seychelles, which comprises 115 islands in all.

I had expected a flat island. But Mahe and many other islands of the Seychelles are actually mountains or hills cloaked in dense green rain forests that rise steeply out of the Indian Ocean. In Mahe a white beach surrounds the base while a large portion of the city looks down from the two mountain ranges, Morne Seychellois and Trois Freres. Both are around 3,000 ft high. The Mahe airport has been built on land reclaimed from the sea. As we stepped into the car I heard the radio announcement: "This is FM Paradise." Seychelles is said to be the original site of Eden. Or perhaps it is rather like what one expects paradise to be. I looked about me and decided that it could be either. I had come across very few places as naturally beautiful as this enchanting island.

As we went up the steep road with hairpin bends I marvelled at the lush green trees all around, some of them forming a shady canopy overhead. I could recognize some of them - mango, jackfruit, papaya, guava and a profusion of banana trees, many of them heavily laden with fruits. There were many others whose names I did not know. Flaming gulmohur, golden laburnum, pink and yellow oleander, yellow and scarlet hibiscus with frilly-edged petals and milk-white frangipani overlapped the green; as did the showers of bougainvillea in pink, orange, white and magenta. A breathtaking riot of colour!

Much of the earlier history of Seychelles is lost in the mists of time. The first recorded landing took place in 1609 when an English East India Company ship with an expedition sailed in. After that there were others, mainly pirates who are said to have buried their treasures which people look for even now. And some other travelers who landed here for some reason or the other, possibly curiosity about the lonely and beautiful island.

The island of Mahe is 27 km long and 8 km at its widest. Most of it is covered with rainforest and forms part of the national park. There are many beautiful beaches. Our hotel was on the Beau Vallon Beach, a gorgeous 3-km crescent shaded by tall coconut palms and the voluminous takamaka trees, special to Seychelles. The wood of the takamaka is mostly used for making furniture.

A big green lizard with red dots peered down inquisitively from the wall as we walked along the long corridor, looking for our room. "It's a gaeko, quite harmless," assured the bellboy, "It eats mosquitoes." The sugary white sands touched the back of the hotel and the sea was just a few steps away. In fact you stepped right on to the beach from the rear veranda. It looked as though the breakers might roll in through the dining room windows any moment!

The next morning I was on my way to Victoria, the quaint capital of Seychelles, said to be one of the tiniest cities in the world. Nestling in the shadow of Trois Freres, it houses the only airport and seaport in Seychelles. The place was originally known as L'Etablissement de Roi, later renamed after the British queen. I passed by clusters of buildings as I walked up the rocky path. At one of the bends there was an awesome view of the harbour. A few more bends and I was at the city centre with its wide streets and smart office buildings. At the crossroads of the two main streets stands the Clock Tower, built in 1903 as a tribute to Queen Victoria. That was when Seychelles became a "Crown colony". Close to it is a tiny porcelain statute of the queen.

I walked along the Independence Avenue passing the colonial-style Law courts. Another popular landmark on the same road is the *Pirates Arms*, a popular rendezvous for meetings and drinks. It is always full of people. Another turn took me to the market place. Apart from shops there are stalls set up in the shade of trees, selling colourful pareos, hats and bags; toys and curios made of shell, coral, coconut husks and other local products. Seychelles has three official languages, English, French and Creole, so communication is not a problem. I looked curiously at whiskey bottles stuffed with red and green chillies.

"What are those?" I asked curiously.

"Hell-fire," came the prompt answer.

I blinked, somewhat taken aback by the name. A lady standing next to me smiled and said, "It's what they call the local chilli sauce. Tastes delicious with fish."

The fish market, a few steps away, teemed with people in various stages of examining, cutting and buying fish as they spoke nineteen to the dozen, mostly in Creole. There were red snappers and tuna; sailfish and bonito; octopus, considered a great delicacy, and many others - all of them glistening with brine. One of the locals told me the names of the fish being sold or I wouldn't have known what they were called. Expert hands filleted, chopped or grated them at incredible speed amidst a constant flow of jokes and chatter. Everything seemed informal and everybody seemed to know everybody!

Close to the market there are several eating joints. Creoles are said to be great cooks, specializing in fish dishes. I entered one and glanced at the menu. The offers included tuna steaks, grilled red snapper, smoked sailfish, grated shark *satini* and octopus curry – all of them packed with spices and smothered in 'hellfire'. I opted for a piece of snapper curried in coconut which tasted great. Apart from fish there was a wide choice of local vegetarian delicacies – breadfruit baked in coconut husk and served with butter; grated green mango salad; and mixed fruit dishes comprising papaya, jamalac, guava and passion fruit to round off a meal in lieu of dessert.

As I walked into the next alley I heard lively feet-tapping music emerging from one of the houses. "Is it the *sega* about which I've heard so much?" I asked one of the elderly passers-by. I had already discovered that the people of Seychelles are friendly, informal and helpful, ever ready to answer questions and pass on bits of information.

"Yes, it is," he answered promptly.

"I thought it is always played on the banjo tambourine and the fiddle? This sounds to me rather like the keyboard," I asked, puzzled.

"It *is* mostly keyboard and the electric guitar these days," he agreed, "One has to keep up with the times, you see."

Both sega and moutia are dances of African origin. The moutia is often accompanied by chants. He also told me that some musicians still play traditional music to the accompaniment of bom, zez, moulumba, tamtam and tambour.

After taking a look at the Bicentennial Monument or Trwa Zwazo, a striking sculpture built to commemorate 200 years of settlement on the islands, I walked up to the old port where fishing boats lay huddled along the little jetty and inter-island schooners were parked side by side. Although Victoria is the only town in Mahe, there are several delightful villages along the coast – Cascade, Anse, Aux Pins and others. Some of these consist of no more than a few scattered houses, a general store, a community centre, a police station and perhaps a church.

Seychelles is a real paradise for those interested in water sports. Apart from snorkeling scuba diving and deep sea diving there is provision for water-skiing, paragliding and windsurfing. All the islands are fringed by coral reefs. One can see them and the fascinating, colourful kaleidoscope of the entire marine life from glass-bottom boats that go out to the sea every day. These boats have panels in the hull through which one can watch the underworld while gliding over it. For those who can afford it, there are luxury yachts and windsurfers for hire, promising an experience out of this world.

For the keen climbers there is the National Park atop the Mor ne Seychellois. It has no motor road and has to be tackled on foot. Despite the steep climb and a long walk within the dense rainforest, the view from up there is said to be well worth the effort. You are likely to need a guide if you decide to explore the Congo Rouge trail. More than 40% of the land area in the Seychelles is set aside as national parks or nature reserves. These include two World Heritage sites – the Aldabra Atoll and Vallee de Mai. Marine national parks are located at Baie Ternay and Port Launey in Mahe, amongst others.

Island hopping is a delightful experience in the Seychelles. There are little 20-seater planes that have regular flights to Praslin, the island next in size to Mahe. It takes just 15 minutes. Other islands have to be reached by boats or helicopters. We took a flight to Praslin. The hushed silence of the Vallee de Mai as we drove through the green canopy overhead comprising coconut palms and the regal *coco de mer*, nearly 100- feet-tall, seemed to take us back in time. Praslin is the only place in the world where the unique coco de mer grows. There are 'masculine' and 'feminine' trees and replicas of the huge nuts with its intriguing shape are on sale everywhere. We went on to La Digue by boat. We remained on the deck and though we were drenched by the splashing breakers it was a trip to remember! La Digue with its quaint bullock carts and its unique Vev Reserve with hundreds of ancient giant sea-turtles crawling about, was again a trip to another time and place.

One of the experiences that stand out in my memory is a bus ride from the city center to the Beau Vallon. All buses charge a flat rate of three Seychelles rupees, no matter what the route or destination. The bus I got into was chockfull of men carrying fruits and vegetables; housewives carrying fish, dusters, brooms and babies; school children carrying satchels; youngsters carrying books and music. There were no cell phones, no laptops but plenty of chatter and laughter. Everyone tried to accommodate the others. Complete strangers volunteered to carry babies from mothers who were standing. Those seated took the heavy bundles from those standing as a matter of course. There was no pushing or pulling, no arguments, no confusion and no frayed tempers. And yet the bus was literally bursting at the seams! I realized then that Seychelles is called paradise not just because of the way it looks but because the inhabitants still believe in human values and the simple joys of life.

Part - II

In the Land of the Singing Waves

It is a crisp January morning.

We are at Tranquebar, a sleepy town nestled in the Coromandel coast, 150km south of Pondicherry. Tarangambadi, its original name, means *the land of the singing waves*.

Nearly four hundred years ago a group of Danish sailors happened to land at this picturesque coastal town that had been the domain of the Cholas and the Pandyas between the 10th and 14th century. When they arrived it was under the reign of the Thanjavur king Vijaya Raghunatha Nayak . The sailors were charmed by the strategic location of the place which seemed an ideal trading post. In November 1620 Ove Gjedde, the Danish captain, signed a treaty with Ragunath Nayak, on behalf of the Danish king Christian IV. The treaty allowed the Danish to build a fort and export pepper and other spices to Denmark. They renamed the town Tranquebar and called the fort Fort Dansborg. The Danes ruled over Tranquebar until 1845 when they sold it to the British. During this period the place became a major commercial hub when the Danes had trade relations with the Arabs and the Portuguese as well.

Incidentally, this windy beach town is the only remaining pocket of Danish culture in India. The whole area has a fascinating feel of washed out old world charm. As it is a small place we decide to explore it on foot. 'Landporten', as the Town Gate is called in Danish, forms part of the fortifications that were built around Tranquebar in the 1660's. In 1791 the original gate was destroyed and the existing one constructed in its place. Apart from the fort on the seashore, the churches and the old monuments are all reminders of the Danish heritage.

Some of the old houses still retain a touch of Dutch glory. You can almost imagine what the town must have looked like during its hey days when you look at the Stucco walls, pillars, verandahs, carriage porches and arched entrance pillars which are distinctly Danish. Along the King Street is a memorial where the Danes had first landed. Three of the churches here are the oldest and most important.

We amble across to the pretty, whitewashed New Jerusalem Church. It was built in 1718 after the arrival of the German missionaries when the existing chapel became too small for the growing Christian population. Bartholomaus Zeigenbalg, a Danish missionary, lies buried in this churchyard. The Zion Church with its combination of colonial and Indian architecture, also on the same road, was set up in 1701 and is the oldest Protestant church in India. The Danish cemetery in the nearby Kavalamettu Street has the graves of several Danish colonial officers and tradesmen. Then there is the Tamil Evangelical Lutheran church, particularly popular with tourists.

Finally, we are at Fort Dansborg which faces the coast. The construction of this fort started soon after the Danes signed the agreement. It was built by Ove Gjedde with the help of local laborers in Danish style. The fort is the second largest Danish fort after Kronborg, which had inspired Shakespeare's immortal tragedy Hamlet. Until the end of the 17th century it was mainly used as a residence and also for storing things. But the subsequent increase in population prompted the people to move out and occupy surrounding areas.

Though small, the fort offers a lot of interesting reading material and artifacts belonging to the Danish East India Company. These include Porcelain ware, Danish manuscripts, Glass objects, Chinese tea jar, Steatite lamps, Decorated terracotta articles, figurines, lamps, Stone Sculptures, Swords, Daggers, Spears, figurines made of mortar, Megalithic Urn and some Chola period utensils, among others. There is also the sea-facing Masilamani Nathar temple which is said to have been built by King Maravarman Kulasekara Pandian in 1306. Despite the Danish occupation and the wave of conversion that followed when most of the existing population were converted to Christianity, the temple still stands on the shore braving the winds.

But the best part of Tranquebar is its gorgeous beach with its clean, silky sand full of pretty shells, parts of the fort walls that still remain after the 2004 Tsunami and the wild, turbulent sea beyond. What we like best is the fact that there are very few tourists and no inevitable garbage or clutter caused by crowds.

We are told that the best place to have a meal/stay overnight is a resort known as Bungalow on the Beach, run jointly by Neemrana and Tamil Nadu tourism. The best part of the resort is its view of the beach with the Masilamani Nathar temple to the left and the Fort to the right. In addition to the spacious dining hall meals are also served on the balcony where the view is an added bonus. The cool and refreshing breeze soon drives off the feeling of exhaustion and make us look forward to a really decent lunch.

We return to the beach once again and find a place to sit down on one of the broken walls. We remain there until twilight to watch the gorgeous sunset before driving back to Pondicherry.

Before the Cosmic Dancer

We are at Chidambaram, located 235 km from Chennai, before the famous temple dedicated to Lord Siva. The place used to be known as Thillai as it was once full of thillai trees, a species of the mangrove tree. The first reference to this temple is found in the Skanda Purana. According to legends, it was first constructed by a king named Shveta Varman who was cured of leprosy by bathing in the sacred pond in the thillai forest way back in the 1st or the 2nd century. Some of the temple structures depicting the thillai trees are said to belong to the 2nd century. Shveta Varman is said to have witnessed the cosmic dance of the Lord and built this temple for the worship of Nataraja. But the original structure was subsequently rebuilt and renovated several times by the kings of the Chola dynasty during the 11th, 12th and 13th centuries.

Spread over an area of nearly 40 acres, the temple has a gopuram (tower) on each side and five sabhas or halls - the Cit Sabha, Kanaka Sabha, Deva Sabha, Nritya Sabha and the Raja Sabha. The idol of Nataraja is located in the Kanaka Sabha along with the idol of Parvati, his consort. What makes the temple special is the fact that here Lord Siva is represented as Nataraja, the cosmic dancer, and not as the symbolic Sivalingam.

The eastern gopuram which is 40.8 m high has the 108 dances mudras (poses) of Bharatanatyam carved on it. The western tower has similar carvings too. The northern tower, 42.4 m high is the tallest of all. According to the Sangam classics, Viduvelvidugu Perumtaccan was the chief architect of the Chidambaram temple, being the one who renovated the original structure constructed during the days of the Chola rule.

Chidambaram is said to be one of the special Siva temples that represent the five natural elements. Chidambaram Nataraja represents akasha (ether). The other four are Jambukeswara at Trichy representing water; Ekambareseswara at Kanchipuram represting earth; Arunachaleswara at Thiruvannamalai representing fire and Kalahasti Natham at Kalahasti representing wind.

Another reason why the temple is special is because it is sacred to both Shaivites and Vaishnavites. There is a shrine dedicated to Govindraja or Lord Vishnu adjacent to the main shrine of Lord Siva. It depicts Lord Vishnu reclining on Adisesha, the serpent. Apart from these there are two other shrines dedicated to Karthikeya (Sumramanya) and Ganesha.

The legend of the Chidambaram temple is an interesting one. The story goes that once upon a time a group of rishis (hermits) who believed in the supremacy of rituals resided in the thillai forest. Lord Siva strolled inside the forest one day in the guise of a simple young tapaswi (hermit lad). His radiant looks made the wives of the rishis admire the unknown youth greatly. This made the rishis so jealous that they invoked poisonous serpents by performing some magic rituals. But the tapaswi simply smiled and lifted the snakes, placing them on his matted locks. The enraged rishis invoked a fierce tiger next. The youth just skinned it and put the skin around his waist. Finally they invoked a powerful demon named Muyalakam. But the young tapaswi just froze the demon, stood on its back and performed the dance of eternal bliss or *Ananda Thandava*. Then the arrogant rishis realized who he really was and fell at his feet in complete surrender.

According to the Puranas, Nataraja's cosmic dance of bliss has a special significance. The demon under Nataraja's feet is said to represent ignorance. The fire in his hand signifies that he is the destroyer of all evil. His raised hand signifies that he is the savior of life. The ring at the back represents the cosmos and the drum (damharu) in his hand represents the origin of life.

There is yet another legend associated with the cosmic dance. When Adhisesha, the serpent who makes a bed for Lord Vishnu, heard about Nataraja's Ananda thandava he also felt a great yearning to see it. Lord Siva told him that he would perform the dance for him. Adhisesha took the form of saint Patanjali and reached the thillai forest where he was joined by another saint, Vyagrapathar. According to the Siva Purana, Nataraja performed the cosmic dance for them on the day of the *poosam* star in the Tamil month of *Thai* (January-February). We can see the images of these two saints with their hands folded, worshipping Lord Nataraja, in one of the mandapams (halls).

An interesting anecdote states that this temple was renovated once again in the middle of the 18th century with support from the Dutch merchants who had a trading post in Porto Nuovo nearby. According to an inscription on one of the copper plates inside the temple, they had donated a share of their profits to get this done.

The tank in the temple complex known as the Siva Ganga is said to be the same lotus pond in the original thillai forest where King Shveta Varman was cured of his ailment and his skin took on the hue of gold. The beautifully maintained tank has long flights of steps leading to the water. People are allowed to take a dip in the pond on special occasions only.

It is now time to enter the main temple. Our worship completed, we bid adieu to the Cosmic Dancer with the sun shining brightly overhead.

Legendary Pushkar

Pushkar, seven miles north of Ajmer, is another celebrated place of pilgrimage. According to the Padma purana, the place owes its holiness to two reasons. First, because Brahma performed his famous yajna here and secondly because the sacred river Saraswati flows here in five streams. Pilgrims flock here by the thousands from the 11th day of Kartik to the full moon or Kartik purnima when the water in the Pushkar lake is said to turn into nectar or amrit, thereby assuring the dippers of a place in paradise.

When I stood by the Pushkar Lake one languid October afternoon, there were neither any pilgrims nor cattle. The lake, tranquil and still, reflected a limpid blue

Autumn sky. A kingfisher hovered overhead, its gaze fixed upon the tiny ripples caressed by the playful breeze. For a moment I wondered why there were no pilgrims despite the beautiful weather. Then I recalled the legend of the lake.

The story goes that when Lord Brahma decided to perform a special yajna on earth he could not decide which place to choose because unlike Vishnu and Siva.

There was no temple dedicated to him on earth. As he stood deep in thought the lotus he had picked up for worship suddenly slipped from his hand. He made up his mind then and there that he would perform the yajna wherever the lotus fell. As the lotus touched the earth water began to spout from the spot and it soon turned into a lake. Brahma named the place Pushkar after the lotus.

It was the month of Kartik. Brahma summoned the other deities and sages, giving each of them special duties for the yajna. He himself stood with the pot of amrit (nectar) on his head, waiting for his wife Savitri to arrive. The sacrifice could not commence without the presence of both. But Savitri refused to come because Lakshmi, Parvati and Indrani who usually went with her everywhere were not there to accompany her. Brahma was very angry when he heard it and ordered Indra to find another bride for him immediately. But the only suitable girl Indra managed to find was belonged to the Gujar caste and was not a Brahmin. So how was she to wed Lord Brahma?

In the mean time Brahma was getting quite impatient and livid because the pot of amrit was a very heavy one. Indra solved the problem by dedicating the girl to a cow. Vishnu said that it was a virtual rebirth and Siva named her Gayatri. Brahma married her and the sacrifice commenced. The moment it was over Savitri turned up too. She was so angry to find her husband married to Gayatri that she refused to be pacified by Brahma or anyone else. She left the place in a huff and went up the hill on the north of the lake. Later a temple was built there in her memory which stands there to this day. The pujari of the main Pushkar temple also has to worship at the Savitri temple atop the hill every time.

To get back to the legend, the Pushkar Lake became so holy after Brahma's yajna that anybody taking a dip there was said to make his way straight to heaven, including the worst of criminals! As a result paradise became overcrowded. The deities residing there complained that the earth was getting to be a really sinful place with no one caring about doing one's duty or being honest because everyone knew that one just had to come to Pushkar and take a dip in order to find a place in heaven and live happily ever after. This made Brahma think again. He finally ordained that Pushkar would be holy for just five days in the year, from the 11th day of Kartik until the full moon which followed. So these are the days when the place is really overcrowded.

With the advent of Buddhism Pushkar, like Varanasi and Mathura, became a stronghold of Buddhism and most people forgot the legends. It became a pilgrimage once again at the beginning of the ninth century AD under the Mandor dynasty. It is said that Narhar Rao, a famous Mandor king, was out hunting one day when he felt thirsty. He came to the Pushkar Lake which had become a neglected pool by then and drank from it. He was amazed to find that the white spots on his wrist had vanished at the touch of the water. Sure of the healing power of the lake water, he tried to find out about its forgotten history. After he did he restored the lake by constructing an embankment and built houses around it for people to stay. The five temples at Pushkar are dedicated to Brahma, Savitri, Badri Narayan, Varaha and Siva. The original temples were mostly destroyed by the Mughals. They were reconstructed much later and are comparatively modern.

Apart from its religious significance Pushkar is also important now for its annual cattle fair. Come November and the sleepy town wakes up to the sound of camels, horses, cows and other animals that come in from various parts of the country for the annual cattle fair, one of the largest in Asia. While brisk trade goes on people and tourists gather to enjoy the fun of the fair and the colourful extravaganza which includes various competitions, such as the camel race, and a dip in the holy lake.

Pushkar, almost surrounded by hills on all sides, is a beautiful place to visit. The Nag pahar on the east deserves special mention because it is full of interesting old caves. Many of them are associated with great sages such as Agastya, Kanva and Bhartrihari. Pushkar is mentioned in both our epics, the Ramayana and the Mahabharata. Ram, Lakhsman and Sita as well as the Panch Pandavas are said to have visited it during their wanderings. Pushkar is mentioned in Jahangir's Memoirs too where he states that the cattle fair at Pushkar is the largest in India. The combination of legends and history, scenic beauty and religious sanctity combine to give Pushkar a special aura of its own.

Magical Madikeri

It is a sluggish, cloudy morning. We are on our way to Madikeri, the capital of Coorg and a place known for its calm, cool, peaceful and pollution-free atmosphere. The very word Coorg brings to mind wooded slopes and colourful scenery; coffee and cardamom; black pepper and honey. The landscape is somewhat rugged but the misty mountain ranges that consists of ridge after ridge of lush, green forests reaching out to the bright blue sky is a sight to behold. The road is remarkably smooth and well maintained and we are hardly aware that we have been climbing up steadily. It is easy to understand why the British selected Coorg and continued to occupy it for over a hundred years. They called it 'The Scotland of India'.

Madikeri, the charming capital of Coorg, is located at an elevation of 1525m. As we look around, breathing in the refreshing mountain air, we see the red-tiled bungalows that dot the hillside and a bustling market place at the heart of the city. There are acres and acres of tea and coffee plantation, orange groves, and undulating paths – all in all, a breathtaking view. The place also has a distinct old world charm about it.

Madikeri or Mercara, as it was called earlier, was founded in 1681 by Muddu Raja, a prince from the Haleri dynasty. It was originally called Muddurajakeri and was later shortened to Madikeri. Apart from being one of the most picturesque hill stations in South India it is also the place from where the river Cauvery originates. It is generally believed that Coorg was ruled mainly by chieftains and local princes until the 17th century. A number of inscriptions and copper plates found in different parts of the state make it obvious that it was under different dynasties at different times - the Gangas, Haleris, Kadambas, Cholas, Kongalvas, Changalvas, Hoysalas and Nayakatas being the most prominent ones among them.

It is time to explore the main sights of Madikeri. What I find most charming is a well-tended park in the heart of the city known as the Raja's seat. It is said to be the place from where the kings watched the setting sun along with their queens. The pavilion offers a gorgeous view of towering hills, green valleys full of paddy fields and forests and the road that looks like a curved ribbon lying way down below.

We next visit the Omkareswara temple built by Lingarajendra Wodeyar II in 1820. The temple that has a beautiful tank in front is a mixture of Gothic and Islamic architecture. The Madikeri fort, an imposing structure that can be seen from almost the entire town, was originally built as a mud fort by Mudduraja along with a palace in the 17th century. It was later rebuilt with granite by Tipu Sultan. When the British took over they added a portico and a clock tower to the building. The fort building now houses a prison, a temple, a chapel, a museum and assorted government offices.

There are a number of tombs/memorials of historical importance in Madikeri. There is the Raja's tomb which is a beautiful structure. The others comprise the tombs of Lingarajendra built in 1820 by his son; the tomb of a royal priest Rudrappa built in 1834 and the tombs of two brave soldiers who died fighting with Tipu Sultan.

The next day we make for the Tala-Cauvery, located 44 km away from Madikeri on the slope of the Brahmagiri hills where the Cauvery River originates. It is one of the important sacred places in Karnataka and is always full of pilgrims. The place is marked by a *tirtha kundike* or a tank where the river emerges as a perennial spring and flows underground again, emerging a short distance away. From Tala-Cauvery there are steps leading to the peak of the Brahmagiri from where one can get a panoramic view of the whole place. We are also keen to visit the Abbey falls about which we have heard so much. But the road is so bad that despite being just 7 km from Madikeri not even the local taxis agree to take us there. And they categorically forbid our driver to make the attempt. Anyway, I tell myself philosophically, there should always be something for the next time!

Madikeri does not have an airport; the nearest one is in Mangalore from where one can hire a taxi to get there. However, KSRTC runs a number of AC and non-AC buses from Bangalore to Madikeri which are quite comfortable. But going by car is the most convenient as it takes just under 6 hours to get there and also because it is difficult to find local transport if you want to go sightseeing. Staying is not a problem as there are a number of budget hotels, home-stays, medium range and luxury hotels as well as resorts. But it is always advisable to book in advance as the place could well be full of tourists and pilgrims just when you plan to visit it.

Nainital: A Hill Station Among Lakes

I had always wanted to visit Nainital, a popular summer retreat in north India. Located in the state of Uttaranchal at an altitude of 1,938 meters, it is not too far from Delhi where I lived at the time. So when an official job turned up to visit the place I was really thrilled.

Though said to be uncomfortably crowded during the tourist season, when I landed up there a few weeks before the tourist season commenced the place was as tranquil as heart could wish. The lake, unruffled except for a few rowing boats, was magnificent in its green splendour, reflecting the tall trees all around and the weeping willows touching the still waters. The blue-grey mountain range surrounding it was resplendent with laburnum, gulmohur, jacaranda and silver oak. To me what seemed most appealing was the hushed silence after the noise of Delhi.

The concept of developing "hill stations" came from the British when they came to India. As they sought refuge in the hills during the hot summer months some of them decided to build colonies where they could escape from the heat and dust of the plains. Nainital, however, had a mythological legend about its creation long before it was made into a popular resort.

The story goes that when goddess Parvati wedded Lord Siva despite her father's disapproval, the latter did not invite them her for an important family function.

Parvati, however, went there uninvited but when her father abused Lord Siva, Parvati, unable to bear the pain, dropped down dead. An enraged Siva broke out into a wild dance during which Parvati's body got severed into pieces and scattered all over the earth. Her eyes were supposed to have fallen in Nainital and the place where they fell turned into a lake. Hence the name Naini tal (the eye lake). There is a temple dedicated to Naina Devi (one of Parvati's names) on the bank of the lake.

The more recent story about how the 'hill station' of Nainital came to be built is interesting too, if rather shocking. For a very long time Nainital remained a quiet village tucked away among the hills. There were hardly any roads except for rough tracks. In 1839 a British businessman named Barron lost his way while travelling in the region and is said to have "stumbled upon a large and beautiful lake hidden in the valley of the Gagar range where only local herdsmen lived."

This is how he describes the place in his memoirs: "An undulating lawn.... interspersed with occasional clumps of oak, cypress and other beautiful trees, continues from the margin of the lake for upwards of a mile up to the base of a magnificent mountain standing at the further extreme of this vast amphitheatre. The sides of the lake are also bounded by special hills and peaks which are thickly wooded, down to the water's edge."

Barron decided to give up his sugar business and build a small colony for Europeans on the lakeside – a settlement later destined to become one of the best-loved hill stations of India. But it was not easy to acquire land just there. The local people who still considered the lake to be sacred because it held the eyes of Parvati had no desire to give up their homeland to a foreigner. So Barron resorted to a trick to get hold of the land. The land around the lake belonged to a local chieftain named Nar Singh. Barron made friends with him and lured him into his boat one evening. He had already found out that Nar Singh could not swim and was extremely scared of the water. Barron rowed him to the middle of the lake, more than 150 meters deep, and told him that unless he surrendered his entire property, he would throw him in. A terrified Nar Singh is said to have signed off his claim to the land in Barron's pocket book on the rocking boat.

Barron built his own home, Pilgrim Cottage, by the lake soon after. Other Europeans followed. By 1845 there were several houses there. Before long there was an army cantonment, a church, a hospital and a club house. The holiday bungalows soon became a permanent township. The town centered round a level stretch called the "Flats" which served as a parade ground. The Sunday morning congregation gathered there after church with the military band entertaining the residents and visitors in the evening. The Flats, a familiar sight in the Hindi films of the 1060s continues to be the centre of activities even now. Though there were no bands playing when I passed by I saw crowds of young people playing games and enjoying themselves.

I was particularly keen to visit Nainital because of Jim Corbett, born there in 1875. He had spent his youth tramping the local forest trails and mountain ranges, shooting several man-eaters. A poorly-paid railway employee, Corbett often helped the impoverished village folks with money and enjoyed a close rapport with them. A local youth pointed out Gurney House, his summer home. The locals still

Think of him with fond reverence.

The lake being the main attraction of Nainital, boating and yachting were favourite pastimes during the British era. The Boat Club was a particularly elite set-up where even Jim Corbett, despite being British, was refused membership because he was merely the son of a postmaster, not grand enough to qualify as a member. Our local guide said that the Kingfisher Yachting Competition held during the third week of

June every year attracts a lot of tourists even now. My friend had also accompanied me and we enjoyed our boat ride on the lake although I shuddered when I remembered that the lake was supposed to be more than 150 feet deep! My friend whose home is in the hills was not nervous, though.

Once my official work was done we went off to check out some of the local sights – the Cheena Peak, the Botanical Garden, St. John's Church, one of the oldest buildings in Nainital, the British Cemetery and the vintage point of "Dorothy's Seat" built by an Englishman named Kellet in memory of his wife. We took the ropeway from the Mall to reach the View Point from where we not only got a panoramic view of the city but also a glimpse of the spectacular Himalayan snow range and the Tibetan borders. Luckily there were binoculars for hire which made it possible. Unfortunately we could not make it to the Hanumangarh temple, said to be a wonderful place for viewing the sunset as time was running short.

Other places close to Nainital include Bhim Tal and the Naukuchia Tal, both of them beautiful lakes.

It was time to go souvenir-hunting. There were attractive handloom products displayed at the shops and also local woollens – shawls and jerseys – known for their warmth. But what I liked best were the candles made locally. There was a breathtaking variety of them in captivating colours and delightful designs from which we picked up several. Then my friend had to leave on some urgent work and I was on my own.

It was dusk and I decided it was time to call it a day. Walking along the road by the lake I saw the setting sun touch the emerald waters with red and gold. The myriad shades of green foliage grew darker matching the growing darkness of the sky. It was a breathtakingly beautiful sight! I realized that it was during moments like these that one feels really close to nature and being alone does not necessarily mean being lonely.

The Shelter of Two-and-a-half Days

Not many people visiting Ajmer for the first time know about the existence of an exquisite mosque complex, not far from the famous Darga Shareef, popularly known as Adhai-din-ka-jhopda. I had heard of it by chance. But I too might have passed it by when I finally made it to the Darga Shareef after a hectic round of sight-seeing, had I not learnt that it was really something special. As we trudged along the narrow path with the languid rays of the setting sun on our face and a haze of dust beneath aching feet, I wondered if it was really worth the trouble. But when I faced the flight of steep and wide stairs at the foot of the hillock where the jhopda stood, deserted and still, I was really glad that I had made it. It was one of the most beautiful monuments I have ever come across. And certainly one of the most imposing.

The jhopda consists of a huge quadrangle cloistered on all four sides. Inside there is a front screen wall of seven pointed arches. According to archaeologists, it was originally a famous seat of Sanskrit learning, containing within the quadrangle a huge temple. This is evident from the large number of figures representing Hindu gods and goddesses excavated from the area. And also from the numerous inscriptions found among the ruins. Most of them are now in the local Rajputana Museum, including the panels containing the inscriptions.

According to tradition when Muhammad Ghori was passing by Ajmer, he was struck by the beauty of the place. He ordered that a mosque should be built there so that he might offer his prayers when he returned after two and a half days. That gave the place its name. Whether they succeeded in keeping the time schedule or not, the original structure was eventually transformed by the end of the 12th century AD into one of the finest and largest specimens of the early mosque. According to another tradition, the name was given by the fakirs (Muslim hermits) who made it their temporary abode when they visited Ajmer. Some other Sufi saints feel that the name signifies the temporary state of man's life on earth, which is no more than a shelter of two-and-a-half days.

The original pillars and the roof of the pre-Muslim structure were allowed to remain although many of the original carvings were defaced. A screen of remarkable beauty was constructed which forms the front of the present mosque, surrounded further by lofty cloisters with a tower at each corner of the quadrangle. This mosque belongs to the same period as the mosque at Qutub Minar. As one of the historians puts it, "...the whole of the exterior (of the jhopda) is covered up with a network of tracery so finely and delicately wrought that it can only be compared to a fine lace."

Among the stone tablets excavated within the jhopda, there are two that contain fine inscriptions from two popular Sanskrit dramas, *Harakeli Natak* and *Lalita Vigraharaja Natak*, both belonging to the middle of the 12th century AD. The first was composed by Vigraharaja, the famous Chauhan king and the second by his court poet Somadeva. These slabs are in the Ajmer museum now along with more than a hundred architectural pieces. These include pillar-shafts, *smalakas*, *Krittimukhas* and other decorative carvings, all of them excavated from different places around the Adhai-din-ka-jhopda. Even now many such pieces lie scattered all over the place.

Some of the interesting medieval sculptures unearthed include figures of rare deities and nakshatras such as Magha, Purva-Phalguni, Uttar-Phalguni, Hasta, Chitra, Swati, Vishakha and so on with their names delicately carved below each figure. Another piece of broken wall has a Nataraja doing the tandava dance, trident in hand, finely carved inside a niche. The Nataraja is accompanied by his two attendants, Nandi and Bhringi. Other figures include one of Goddess Chamunda and another of Kuvera standing on a full-blown lotus, as well as numerous Vishnu, Siva and Shakti figures.

What really stands out about the place is the aura of tranquility which surrounds it. Despite the fact that it is within the heart of the city, it wears a calm, deserted air with just the occasional call of birds to break the silence. One can easily understand why it was made a site for temple and mosque. It is ideally suited for prayers and quiet meditation. Standing in the shade of the lofty structure, away from the bustle, din and pollution of the noisy city, it is easy to realize and believe that there is a God above.

About the Author

Swapna Dutta has been writing books for children for nearly five decades with over 50 titles to her credit, including translations, published by Hachette, Orient Blackswan, Scholastic, Shristi, Children's Book Trust, National Book Trust, Pan Macmillan and others. Two of her books have been listed by White Ravens (International Youth Library, Munich) and 17 in Good Reads. Her contribution to magazines includes Children's World, Target, The Bookbird (USA), The School Magazine (Australia), Scottish Home & Country (UK) and Folly (UK). She worked as Editorial Consultant with Target (Living Media), was Assistant Editor, Limca Book of Records; and Deputy Editor, Encyclopaedia Britannica, India, between 1988 and 2002. Dutta has presented papers on various aspects of children's literature at national and international conferences (including IBBY) and has won several prizes and awards for her work and a National Fellowship from the Ministry of Culture.

Printed in the USA
CPSIA information can be obtained
at www.ICGtesting.com
LVHW091637080424
776714LV00025B/226